Viking Adventure

By the Author

The Donkey Cart
Riding the Pony Express*
The Secret Valley*
Surprise for a Cowboy
A Ranch for Danny
Johnny Hong of Chinatown
Song of St. Francis
Eagle Feather*
Star of Wild Horse Canyon*
Down the Mississippi
Squanto, Friend of the Pilgrims*
The Poppy Seeds
White Sails to China*
The Sword in the Tree*
John Billington, Friend of Squanto
Old Charlie*
Ghost Town Treasure*
Pirate's Promise
Stories of Favorite Operas
The Valentine Cat
Three-Dollar Mule*
A Tree Is a Plant
The Sugar Pear Tree
Benito
The Ring and the Fire
What Makes a Shadow?*
Viking Adventure*
Indian Hill
St. Valentine's Day

*Available in paperback from Scholastic Book Services

Viking Adventure

by Clyde Robert Bulla

Illustrated by Douglas Gorsline

SCHOLASTIC BOOK SERVICES
NEW YORK · TORONTO · LONDON · AUCKLAND · SYDNEY · TOKYO

Copyright © 1963 by Clyde Robert Bulla. This edition is published by Scholastic Book Services, a division of Scholastic Magazines, Inc., by arrangement with Thomas Y. Crowell Company, Inc.

13 12 11 10 9 8 7 6 5 4 3 2   7 8 9/7 01/8

Printed in the U.S.A.

To Kimmis

Contents

Viking Adventure

1

Olaf the Strong

Long ago the land of Norway was a Viking land. The sea about it was a Viking sea.

They were a bold, brave people, the Vikings. The sea was their road to adventure, and they loved it. But they loved the land, as well.

Olaf the Strong loved both sea and land. Once he had sailed in Viking ships. He had fought in far places. Then a wound had put an end to his fighting days. He had come home to his farm in the south of Norway.

Olaf took a wife, and children were born to them.

The first two children were daughters. Their names were Helga and Erna.

The last child was a son. His name was Sigurd.

The mother taught the daughters. She taught them to cook and make cloth and sew.

The father taught the son.

When Sigurd was three, Olaf said, "It is time you learned to swim."

He took the boy down to the sea. He threw him into the water.

The sea was cold. The water was deep. Sigurd sank and came up and almost sank again.

"Swim!" said his father.

Sigurd pushed with both hands. He kicked as hard as he could—and he began to swim.

His father pulled him out of the water. "Now

you see how it is done," he said. "Next time you will do better."

As soon as Sigurd could swim and dive, he learned to ride horseback. He learned to throw a spear and shoot a bow and arrow.

"You must be strong," said his father.

On Olaf's farm there were three houses and three barns. He and his family lived in the biggest house. Servants lived in the other two. The barns were for the horses, cattle, and sheep.

The houses and barns were built together like a small, square town. In the middle was a square of grass, and a tall ash tree grew there.

Olaf tied a rope to a branch of the ash tree. Every day he told Sigurd to climb the rope.

Sigurd climbed up and down. He learned to climb hand over hand, without using his feet.

Every day his father told him to run.

Sigurd ran around and around the square. He ran until he was tired.

Sometimes Olaf told him to jump off the roof of the house.

The first time Sigurd looked down from the roof he said, "It is too far."

"You must not be afraid," said his father. "Land with your head and arms forward. Now!"

Sigurd jumped. He landed as his father had told him to do.

"See?" said Olaf. "Was it too far?"

Sigurd stood up. He was not hurt. "No," he said. "It was not too far."

After that he never feared to jump off the roof.

But as he grew older, he began to ask himself questions. Why must there be so many lessons? Why must he leave his warm bed in the morning to run around the square? Why was there so little time for him to play games with his sisters?

One day his father was teaching him to fight in battle. Olaf had had a small sword and shield made for Sigurd. Sigurd was learning to use them.

"Draw your sword! Charge!" his father said over and over.

The day was warm. The lesson had gone on for a long time.

Olaf looked into the boy's hot face.

"Rest," he said.

Sigurd was so surprised he almost let his sword fall. His father had never told him to rest before.

"The lessons are hard," said Olaf, "and you cannot see why there must be so many. Is this not so?"

Sigurd said nothing.

"Some day you *will* see," said his father.

2
The Feast

On a winter night there was a feast in Olaf's hall. Olaf's friends came from nearby farms. Some walked over the snow. Some came in sleds pulled by horses.

Sigurd and his sisters were so excited they could not keep still. They ran from the hall to the kitchen and back. Their dog Ho was with them. Once he ran under their feet, and they all fell down.

"Children, children!" said their mother. But she did not scold them, because it was such a happy time.

Olaf and his wife sat at the long table with their friends. Servants brought food and drink. They brought dishes of roasted meat. They brought jugs of wine. They brought honey bread with white cheese and sweet butter.

The children had a small feast of their own. They ate by the fire. Their table was a butter tub. Ho lay near them. When he barked, they gave him bites of food.

They watched the people at the long table.

The girls looked at the gold rings on the women's hands.

"See the pins in the hair of that lovely lady," said Erna. She asked her sister, "Do you think the pins are gold?"

"Yes," said Helga. "Look at her, Sigurd. Isn't she beautiful?"

Sigurd was looking at his father.

Olaf was at the head of the table. He sat in the dragon chair. It was a chair of oak, carved with many dragons. Sigurd had touched the carved wood, but he had never sat in the chair. Only the master of the house sat there.

Olaf sat like a king.

Sigurd felt happy and proud when he looked at his father.

The children were sent to bed early. They slept

in the loft above the hall. The girls' bed was on one side of the loft, Sigurd's was on the other.

Sigurd had wanted to stay up. He knew that stories were told at every feast. He wanted to hear the stories.

He fell asleep and woke again. A woman was talking in the hall below. He could hear some of the words. She was telling a ghost story.

Sigurd got out of bed and listened at the top of the stairs. Still he could not hear all the words.

He went down the stairs until he could hear better.

The woman said, "The ghost gave a cry and flew away and never came back." That was the end of her story.

One of the men looked up. "I think the ghost did come back," he said. "I see him now."

The others looked and saw Sigurd on the stairs. Some of them laughed to see him sitting there in his short nightshirt.

"Sigurd!" said his mother. "Back to bed!"

But Olaf held out his hands.

Sigurd went to him.

"Do you think you are old enough to sit up and hear the stories?" asked Olaf.

"I am eight," said Sigurd.

"That is true," said Olaf. "Sit here, then. I have a story to tell. You are old enough to hear it."

Sigurd sat at his father's feet.

Olaf began. He told the story of his life. He told how he had gone to sea when he was young. He told of his friend Gorm and their adventures in strange lands.

The lands had such names as Iceland, Scotland, Ireland, Spain . . .

"There was a battle on the shore of Ireland," said Olaf. "A wild man came into the fight. Seven feet tall he was, and he swung his sword left and right. He wounded me here in the side. It was my good friend Gorm who saved my life. He cared for me until I was able to come home. And here I have stayed ever since."

He said to Sigurd, "Still awake? My story did not put you to sleep?"

"Tell more," said Sigurd.

"My story is over," said Olaf.

"Tell about the other lands," said Sigurd.

"Some day," said Olaf.

"Have you gone farther than anyone else has ever gone?" asked Sigurd.

"No," said Olaf. "Some have gone much farther."

"Who?" asked Sigurd.

"One was Leif, son of Erik," said his father.

"Did you know him?" asked Sigurd.

Some of the others began to laugh.

"No, I did not know him," said Olaf. "He lived a hundred years ago. A hundred years, and more. His home was in Greenland."

"I know about Greenland," said Sigurd. "It is far beyond Iceland."

"Yes," said Olaf, "and Leif sailed even beyond Greenland. He found a land there, and he named it Wineland."

Sigurd waited for him to go on. He asked, "Why did he name it Wineland?"

"Tell him the story, Olaf," said one of the men.

"Another time," said Olaf. "Now to bed, my son."

Sigurd went back up the stairs. He lay in bed, thinking.

Many times his father had told him, "You must not be afraid. You must be strong."

Now Sigurd knew why. Adventures would come to him as they had come to his father. When they came, he must be ready. He must be brave. He must be strong.

3

The Land
Across the Sea

On the day after the feast, Olaf called Sigurd into the hall.

Sigurd thought it was time for his lesson. He took his sword and shield down off the wall.

"Wait," said his father. "Come here."

He sat down in the dragon chair. Sigurd sat near him.

"Last night you asked for the story of Leif," said Olaf. "I could not tell it then. Others were waiting to tell *their* stories. But you shall hear it now."

He began the story:

"You know that Greenland is far to the west. Leif believed there were lands beyond Greenland. He wanted to find them. He bought a ship, and he and his men set sail. Soon they saw land.

"It was a land of ice and snow. They sailed on to the south, and there they found another land. It was flat and rocky. Leif and his men soon sailed from there. They sailed to the south until they came to another land — the most beautiful land they had ever seen."

"Wineland!" said Sigurd.

"Yes, Wineland," said his father. "The shore was low. The sand was clean and bright. There were hills and trees and grass. Clear streams ran into the sea, and fish leaped in the streams. The sky was fair. The sun was warm.

"The men found vines among the trees. There were grapes on the vines. You know that wine is made from grapes. This is why Leif gave the land the name of Wineland. He and his men built houses. They lived that winter in Wineland. In the spring they sailed for home.

"Leif wanted his family and friends to know of the beautiful land. He wanted them to see it, too. But it was not a happy year for his people. There was sickness among them. There were quarrels. Leif never went back to the land he had found."

Sigurd asked, "Is that the end of the story?"

"Yes," said Olaf.

"What of the beautiful land?" asked Sigurd. "Do people go there now?"

"No," said Olaf. "People have lost the way."

"Can no one find it?" asked Sigurd.

"Once I hoped to find it," said Olaf. "Last night I spoke of my friend Gorm. Do you remember?"

"Yes," said Sigurd. "He was the friend who saved your life."

"Gorm and I hoped to find the beautiful land together," said Olaf. "It was a dream we had. But we were young. We had no ship. We had no crew of men. Now Gorm is gone—I don't know where. The dream is gone as well."

He was quiet for a while. Then he said, "We have talked long enough, my son. It is time for your lesson."

Out in the square, Sigurd practiced with his sword and shield.

"Draw your sword — shield high!" said his father. "Charge — shield low!"

Sigurd's thoughts were on the story he had heard. He thought of Leif and the land across the sea.

His father's voice came to him. "Mind what I say!"

Sigurd stood still. "I—I did not hear."

"You did not listen," his father said in anger, but the anger was quickly gone from his eyes. "I know. You are tired of fighting the air with your sword. You are tired of charging at nothing. Is this not so, my son?"

"Sometimes," said Sigurd.

"Then you shall share your lessons," said his father.

"Share them?" said Sigurd.

"Yes," said his father. "It is time you fought someone real."

"Who?" asked Sigurd.

"We shall see," said his father.

4
Rolf

Sigurd had many cousins. Most of them lived a long way off, near the village of Kon. Some of them he had never seen.

Toward the end of winter, Olaf set out for Kon. He left on horseback. He was gone seven days.

When he came home, he was not alone. A boy rode beside him on a small, black pony.

Sigurd ran out to meet them.

His father said, "Come, my son. Speak to your cousin Rolf."

Sigurd spoke to the boy. "Well met."

The boy said nothing. His face was not friendly.

Inside the house, Olaf told Sigurd, "Your cousin will be here for a while."

He left the two boys alone together.

Rolf took off his fur cap and coat. He walked

about the hall, looking at the spears and swords and shields on the wall.

He put his hand on the dragon chair.

Sigurd said quickly, "That is my father's chair. Only he sits in it."

"I don't want to sit in it," said Rolf. He was looking at Sigurd. "How old are you?"

"Near to nine," said Sigurd. "How old are you?"

"Past ten," said Rolf. "How tall are you?"

"As tall as you, I should think," said Sigurd.

"That may be," said Rolf, "but I have more meat on my bones. Do you think you are as strong as I am?"

"That may be," said Sigurd.

"We'll soon find out," said Rolf. "Do you know why I am here?"

"My father gives me lessons," said Sigurd. "You and I will have lessons together."

"That's true, in a way," said Rolf, "but do not think that I am here to be your friend. I'm here to fight you."

The next day they fought for the first time. They

Gorsline

fought out in the square with shields and wooden swords.

Sigurd's father watched. Some of the servants watched, too.

Rolf came at Sigurd in a rush. Sigurd put up his shield, but he was too late. Rolf had already given him a whack on the head.

Sigurd tried to step aside. Rolf gave him a whack in the ribs.

Sigurd had to work hard to keep from being struck again. He worked so hard with his shield that he could not strike back.

After a while his father said, "Enough."

The boys put away their swords. Sigurd thought he had fought a poor fight. He wished his father had not been watching.

But Olaf said, "You have not done badly. Rolf is older. He has been fighting longer. You will learn from him."

Sigurd did learn. He learned Rolf's tricks. Soon he knew how to fight back.

Sometimes the boys wrestled. At first it was easy

for Rolf to win. But again Sigurd learned. Soon Rolf had to work hard to throw him down.

Once they wrestled for an hour. Neither could win. They sat down to rest. "For a boy, you are strong," said Rolf.

Sigurd laughed. "What are you, a man?"

"I'll be a man long before you are," said Rolf.

"What will you be when you grow up?" asked Sigurd.

"A shipbuilder," said Rolf.

"I'm going to sea when I grow up," said Sigurd. "My father had great adventures. I want to have adventures, too."

"You should have lived in the old days," said Rolf. "My father says the days of our great adventures are over."

"There are still adventures," said Sigurd. "Think how it would be to sail to all the far places—Scotland, Ireland, Spain, Wineland—"

"Wineland?" said Rolf.

"It is the land found by Leif, son of Erik," said Sigurd. "Don't you know about Leif?"

"I know the story," said Rolf, "but Wineland isn't real. It's only make-believe."

"It isn't make-believe," said Sigurd. "My father says there *is* a Wineland."

"My father says there isn't," said Rolf. "Leif lived a long time ago. He lived a long way from here. For a hundred years people have told stories about him. Now no one knows which ones are true and which ones are make-believe."

"The story about Wineland is true," said Sigurd.

"How do you know?" asked Rolf.

"My father says it is," said Sigurd. "He was going there once."

"He didn't go, did he?" asked Rolf.

"No," said Sigurd.

"Others say they are going," said Rolf, "but no one ever does go."

Sigurd did not answer. But he said to himself, There *is* a Wineland. My father says there is, and I believe my father!

5
Old Bard

Spring came. Rolf went home to work on his father's farm. But the next winter he was back, and the winter after that.

He and Sigurd rode together in the hunt. They practiced with bows and arrows, and swords and spears. They wrestled, and they ran races.

"Father told me I would learn from you," said Sigurd. "I *have* learned. I wish you could be here all the time."

Yet Rolf kept saying, "I am only here to fight you." He never was Sigurd's friend.

The winter Sigurd was twelve, his father said, "Your cousin will not be with us this year."

Sea raiders had come from the north. They had made a raid on the village of Kon. They had carried off cattle and sheep, and set fire to the village.

"Rolf is helping build new houses and barns," said Olaf.

Sigurd thought, If raiders came to Kon, they may come here.

He slept with his sword beside him. It was not a wooden sword, but one with a blade of steel.

He went often to the shore to watch for strange ships. Once he saw a dragon ship. He watched to see if it would land, but it sailed on.

He told his father about the ship. "It had a drag-

on's head in front and a dragon's tail behind. There was a row of shields along the side. Do you think it was the raiders' ship?"

"It may have been," said his father. "But the ship sailed on. We are in no danger."

Still Sigurd kept watch.

One night in early spring he woke. The dogs were barking.

He sprang up and put on his clothes. With sword in hand he ran outside.

He climbed the big gate that was always locked at night. He looked over the top.

The night was clear. There was light enough for him to see the dogs. They were near the gate, barking and tearing at something on the ground.

Sigurd climbed over the gate. He shouted at the dogs. When they drew back, he saw a man lying in the road.

"Help!" cried the man. "My horse—"

The big gate opened. Olaf came out. Behind him came servants carrying torches.

They looked at the man in the road.

He was old. His clothes were in rags.

"Do you think he is a raider?" asked Sigurd.

"No," said Olaf. "Let us bring him in."

Two of the servants lifted the old man. They carried him into the house and put him down by the fire.

He began to talk. His voice was gentle.

Sea raiders had come to his village, he said. They had robbed and killed. They had burned the village. He had fled on horseback.

"I wished to find the home of Olaf the Strong," he said, "but I lost my way. When I saw this house, I hoped there were kind people here who might give me a bed for the night. But the dogs came barking. They bit my horse's heels until he threw me off and ran away. My horse—you must help me find him!"

"Why did you seek the home of Olaf the Strong?" asked Sigurd's father.

"I hoped to find a place under his roof," said the old man. "His father was my friend."

"Who are you?" asked Olaf.

"Young Bard, I once was," said the old man. "Old Bard, I am now."

"Bard, the singer of songs?" asked Olaf. "Bard, the teller of tales?"

"You know me?" said the old man.

"My father knew you," said Olaf. "Many times I heard him speak your name."

"Then you are Olaf!" said the old man.

"I am," said Olaf, "and I bid you welcome."

"I give you blessing," said the old man.

Then he cried out, "Will you find my horse?"

Sigurd took a torch and left the house. He waited outside the gate, in the hope that the horse would come.

He heard the sound of hoofs, and he spoke in a quiet voice.

The horse came near. He was old and lame. A large cloth bag hung from the saddle.

Sigurd spoke again. The horse stood still. Sigurd caught his bridle and led him into the barn.

Back in the house, he told the old man, "I have found your horse."

"Was there a bag on the saddle?" asked the old man.

"Yes," said Sigurd.

"Ah!" said the old man, and he smiled. "My books are safe."

6
Tales Before the Fire

Olaf gave Bard a room next to his own. Servants brought food and drink for the old man. They made him a good bed of straw.

In the morning he called for his books.

Sigurd brought him the cloth bag. Bard looked into it. He began to take out books.

"They are all here. They are all safe," he said. "My young friend, I thank you."

Sigurd had never seen so many books before. Most of them were large and thick. Some had covers of leather. Some had covers of wood. One was written on a roll of strong, heavy paper.

"Are there stories in these books?" he asked.

"Yes," said Bard, "and other things that men know."

"Where did the books come from?" asked Sigurd.

"Many places. Some I wrote myself." Bard showed Sigurd a book. "This I wrote. I was young then. My eyes were good, and my hand did not shake."

Sigurd looked into the book. "Are there pictures?"

"No," said Bard.

"Then it would do me no good." Sigurd closed the book.

"You cannot read?" asked Bard.

"No," said Sigurd.

"You can learn," said the old man.

"Not I," said Sigurd. "I am like my father. He was never a man for reading and writing. But it would please me to hear your stories."

"You shall hear them," said the old man.

When he was well and strong again, he began to tell his stories. He told them at night before the fire.

Olaf said to him, "It is good to hear these tales. Stay with me, and I will pay you well for them."

"I will gladly stay and tell my tales, but not for pay," said Bard. "You have given me a good home. I thank you for it."

He called Sigurd to his room one day.

"You have been kind to me," he said. "I have gifts for you, if you will take them."

"What are they?" asked Sigurd.

"The gift of reading," said the old man. "The gift of writing."

Sigurd shook his head. "They are not for me."

"Why do you say that?" asked Bard.

"I am to have a life of adventure," said Sigurd. "Reading and writing take years to learn. I have no time for them."

"They may not take as long as you think," said Bard. "I can teach you. Let me try."

"What is the good?" asked Sigurd.

"Listen to what I say," said Bard. "When a story is told and told again, it does not stay the same. One man leaves off something. Another man puts on something. In a little while no one can say how much of the story is true. But if a man *writes* the story, it is not lost. Others may read it. Even after a hundred years, it is still the same."

"That may be true," said Sigurd, "but *I* have no story to write."

"Would you not like to read what is written in books?" asked Bard.

"Others can tell me what is written in them," said Sigurd.

"If you will not think of yourself, will you think of me?" said Bard. "I have much to write. But I am old. It is hard for me to see my writing. My fingers are stiff. It is hard for me to hold the pen. I need someone young who will be my eyes and my hands."

"My sisters—" said Sigurd.

"I have asked them," said Bard. "They say they are only girls and cannot learn such things. They laugh and run away."

"But how do you know *I* could learn such things?" asked Sigurd.

"You can learn. I feel it. Come here." The old man was sitting at his table. He took up a pen. He dipped it into an ink-cup. "Watch me." On a scrap of paper he wrote a word. "Now—write it after me."

Sigurd took the pen. He tried to write as Bard had done. The ink made an ugly blot on the paper.

He dropped the pen. "You see, I cannot do it!"

He heard his father walking outside.

"I must go," he said. "My father is waiting."

The old man looked down at the pen. His eyes were sad.

Sigurd felt ashamed. He said, "Another day I may try to learn reading and writing."

But the days went by, and he did not try.

7
The Horseman

All that spring there was talk of raiders along the shore. Every day Sigurd watched for them.

One morning he saw a horseman coming toward the house. He stood guard by the gate. He kept his bow and arrow ready.

The horseman came nearer. He rode like a young man, but there was gray in his beard.

"Come no farther!" called Sigurd.

The man held up his hand. "Well met, son of Olaf!"

Sigurd was surprised. "You know me?"

"We have not met before," said the man, "but you are a son of Olaf, that is plain. You have his look." He saw the bow and arrow in Sigurd's hands. "Were you going to stop me with an arrow?"

"Only if you were a raider," said Sigurd.

"I am no raider. I come as a friend," said the man. "Will you run and tell your father that Gorm is here at last?"

"*Gorm,* did you say?" Sigurd gazed at the man. "The friend who saved my father's life?"

"If he has told you so," said the man, "it must be true."

Sigurd ran to the house.

His father was in the doorway. "Where is he? I heard his voice. Gorm!" he shouted.

The two men met in the middle of the square.

"My friend!" said Olaf. "I had thought you were far from here."

"I *have* been far," said Gorm. "It will take long to tell you of the places I have seen."

The men sat together in the hall. Sigurd and his mother and sisters sat near them.

Olaf asked his friend, "Where are your wife and children?"

"Wife and children I have none," said Gorm. "Some day I may find myself a home, but the time is not now. Soon I go on a new adventure."

"Where will it take you?" asked Olaf.

Gorm's eyes were bright. "Remember our dream?"

"What dream is that?" asked Olaf.

"Remember how we talked of going to the land across the sea?"

"How could I forget?" said Olaf.

"Sometimes a dream comes true," said Gorm. "Listen! I met a wealthy trader, young Halfred. He seeks new lands and new wealth, but he does not know much of the sea. We spoke of Wineland. I told him, 'The land is real, and I can find it.' Again and again I told him, until he believed me. Now he is ready with a ship."

"And a crew?" asked Olaf.

"Yes, a crew of a hundred men," said Gorm. "Remember the ships of our young days—ships without decks, and only tents to keep off the snow and rain? This ship has a deck, with rooms below."

"And you will really sail to Wineland?" asked Olaf.

"Yes," said Gorm. "And there is a place for you.

We shall have our dream. We shall walk together on the shores of Wineland."

Olaf looked away.

"Do you hear me?" said Gorm.

"I hear you. I hear you too well," said Olaf. "The dream cannot be."

"It can!" said Gorm. "The ship lies near the town of Torvik, only a day's ride away. I am captain, and you shall sail with me."

"No," said Olaf. "You know my wound. In all these years it has never healed. It will not let me go."

The hall was still for a while.

Gorm said, "I thought this would be a glad time. Now I am sad."

"You must not be sad," said Olaf. "Think of the adventure that will be yours."

"Yes," said Gorm. "A great adventure."

Sigurd had listened. He had heard every word.

He said, "Take me!"

"What?" said Gorm.

"Take me with you," said Sigurd.

Gorm smiled a little. "It is a voyage for a man."

"I am a man—almost. I am thirteen."

Sigurd stood up to show Gorm how tall he was. "I can do a man's work, and—"

"Sit down," said his father. "You are too bold."

Sigurd sat down. He wanted to cry out, "I *must* go!"

But he sat very still, while the men talked and the day went by.

8
Olaf's Answer

In the morning Gorm was ready to go.

Olaf and Sigurd went with him to the gate. He shook their hands and rode away.

Sigurd asked, "Will he come again before he sails?"

"No," said his father. He went into the house.

Sigurd was left alone.

He began to walk. He did not know where he was going, but he kept on until he came to the sea.

He sat under a pine tree and looked out across the water. Sea gulls were crying. The sun was bright on the waves. For half the morning he sat there, thinking.

A voice came to him from far away. His mother was calling him.

He went back to the house.

His mother was at the gate. "You were gone so long," she said. "I thought you had fallen into the sea."

"Mother, you know I can swim," he said.

He went inside. In the hall he found Olaf.

"Father, I have been thinking," he said. "I tried to put the thought out of my mind, but always it came back."

"What are you thinking?" asked Olaf.

"I must go with Gorm," said Sigurd.

"It is no voyage for you," said his father.

"I am strong, and I am not afraid," said Sigurd. "Since you cannot go, let me go in your place."

"You are still a boy," said his father.

"I am thirteen," said Sigurd. "There are many sailors not much older."

"Gorm does not want you," said Olaf.

"So he said. Yet I must ask him one more time," said Sigurd.

"He will say no," said Olaf.

"But if he will have me, then may I go?" asked Sigurd.

Olaf looked into the fire as if he were deep in thought. He said at last, "If he will have you, you may go."

Sigurd's mother had come into the hall. "What is this?" she asked.

"I am going to Torvik," said Sigurd. "I am going to sail with Gorm if he will have me."

"No!" she cried.

"The ride to Torvik will do him no harm," said Olaf. "A servant will go to show him the way."

"I must be there before the ship sails," said Sigurd. "May I go now? May I go quickly?"

"When you wish," said his father.

Sigurd ran up to the loft. He opened the chest by his bed. He took out his better clothes and put them on.

When he went downstairs, there were two horses at the door. One was his pony. The other was for the servant who was to ride with him.

Sigurd's sisters were excited.

"Even if Gorm sends you home," said Helga, "going to Torvik will be an adventure."

"I wish Father would let me ride with you," said Erna.

"It will be late when you reach Torvik," said Olaf. "Stay at the inn tonight." He gave Sigurd a purse. "Here is money enough, and more."

"Thank you, Father." Sigurd tied the purse to his belt.

His mother began to weep.

She was still weeping when he and the servant rode away.

9
The Stone

The sun went down while they were on the road to Torvik. Sigurd kept asking the servant, "Are we nearly there?"

The servant would answer, "A little farther, young master."

They came to Torvik at last. The town was dark and quiet. It smelled of fish and the sea. The servant knew where the inn was. He led Sigurd to it.

Sigurd got off his pony and knocked at the door.

A man looked out. "What do you want?" he asked, and he sounded sleepy and cross.

"A bed for the night," said Sigurd, "for my servant and me."

"A bed for the night? It's but an hour till daylight," said the man. "Come in if you must. Your servant can go to the barn with the horses."

"If it's but an hour till daylight," said Sigurd, "I'll go with my servant."

They went to the barn behind the inn. They led the horses inside and gave them water and hay.

The servant lay down and slept. Sigurd sat in the doorway and waited for day to come.

When the sky was light, he went outside. There were small fishing boats in the harbor, and there was one ship. It was not as long and slim as a dragon ship. It was low and wide, and built to carry a heavy load.

Men were moving about on board. Others had slept on the shore. Some of them were just getting out of their cowskin sleeping bags.

Sigurd asked one of them, "Are you the men who sail with Gorm?"

"We are," said the sailor.

"Where is he now?" asked Sigurd.

"He may be on the ship. He may be at the inn," said the sailor. "Halfred can tell you."

"Where is Halfred?" asked Sigurd.

"There," said the sailor.

A man had come out of the inn. He came down to the harbor, his long blue cloak blowing in the wind. His face was thin. His eyes were dark.

Sigurd spoke to him. "Will you tell me where I may find Gorm?"

The man looked Sigurd up and down. "Why should I tell you?"

"He is my father's friend," said Sigurd. "I must see him before he sails."

"Why?" asked the man.

"Because," Sigurd began, "I wanted—"

"Speak!" said the man.

"I wanted to sail with him," said Sigurd.

"You? On this voyage?" said Halfred. "There is no place on my ship for a boy." He walked away.

Sigurd ran after him. "May I have a chance?"

Halfred looked at him and laughed. It was a short laugh, like the bark of a dog. "So you want a chance? I'll give you a chance. Go and lift the test-stone."

Sigurd stared at him.

"Quick!" said Halfred. "Go and lift it."

Sigurd looked about him. He saw many stones on the ground.

A young sailor had been watching. He said to Sigurd in a low voice, "All who are fit to be seamen must show that they can lift the test-stone."

"Which is the test-stone?" asked Sigurd.

"This one," said the young sailor.

Sigurd looked down at the stone. It was smooth and black and large.

"Well?" said Halfred. "Do you still want to try?"

"Yes," said Sigurd.

A crowd of sailors had gathered.

Sigurd threw off his cloak. He bent down. He put his hands under the stone and tried to lift it.

The stone did not move.

He set his feet far apart. Again he lifted. The stone moved a little.

He closed his eyes. Slowly, with all his strength, he raised the stone. He raised it as high as his knees. He held it there a moment. Then he let it fall.

Some of the men broke into a cheer.

One said, "Well done, son of Olaf!"

It was Gorm, standing with the others. Sigurd had not known he was there. Gorm asked, "Does your father know you are here?"

"Yes," said Sigurd. "He says I may sail with you —if you will have me."

"We have our men," said Halfred.

"Surely we could use one more man to row," said Gorm.

"A man, yes," said Halfred. "Not this boy."

"Yet you told him to take the test," said Gorm.

"I only thought to teach him a lesson," said Halfred. "I did not think he could lift the stone."

"No more did I," said Gorm, "yet he did lift it."

"This boy is too bold," said Halfred. "There is a look on his face that does not please me."

"He has the face of his father, who is my friend," said Gorm. "I say he shall go with us."

"The ship is mine," said Halfred.

"And I am captain," said Gorm. "You chose me so yourself, and even the man who owns the ship does not speak above the captain."

Halfred's face was dark with anger, but he said no more.

Gorm smiled at Sigurd. "I am glad you did not wait. We sail tomorrow."

Sigurd said, "Thank you." He spoke quietly, but he wanted to shout. He wanted to sing. Over and over he said to himself, I am going—I am going!

10
Aron

The ship sailed in the early morning light.

Sigurd was at his place on one of the rowers' benches. He was pulling an oar, along with two other sailors.

Along each side of the ship he could see men hard at work. It took three rowers to pull each of the great oars.

A crowd of people had come to the shore. They were watching the ship sail.

Sigurd's servant was there.

Sigurd looked out over the side of the ship. The servant waved. Sigurd did not wave back. He was too busy with the oar.

He knew the servant would soon be on his way home. He would be riding one horse and leading the other.

The servant would say, when he reached home, "The young master is gone."

Sigurd thought his father and sisters would be happy. He knew his mother would be sad.

A girl on shore called out, "Bring us grapes from Wineland!" and the crowd laughed.

Sigurd asked the man next to him, "Why do they laugh?"

"When we say we are going to Wineland, they do not believe us," said the man. "They think it is a joke."

"Do *you* believe we are going to Wineland?" asked Sigurd.

"Who knows?" said the man. "If I have food and drink and my pay, we can sail to the moon for all I care."

Later Sigurd and Gorm sat in Gorm's room below deck. Sigurd told him what the man had said.

"Most people do not believe we are sailing to Wineland," said Gorm. "They say there is no such land. Some believe we are going to look for treasure. Others think we will sail the seas as pirates."

"But that is not true!" said Sigurd.

"No, it is not true," said Gorm. "You and I know we are sailing to Wineland. A few others know it. The rest must learn."

There were more than a hundred men on board. Sigurd came to know most of them.

There was old Ivar, who could steer the ship almost as well as Gorm. There were Alf and Harald, two tall brothers from the far North. There was Aron, who was not much older than Sigurd.

It was Aron who had shown Sigurd the test-stone. Sometimes they rowed side by side.

On days when the winds were fair, the men did not have to row. They drew the oars inside the ship.

On these days Sigurd and Aron were often together. They walked on deck or sat in one of the small sleeping rooms below. They looked in at the sour old cook, who guarded the barrels and tubs in the storeroom. There were salt fish, beef, and hard bread in the barrels. There were barrels of water too. The tubs held butter and cheese.

Next to the storeroom was an iron firebox filled

with sand. Sometimes the cook made a charcoal
fire on the sand and cooked a great kettle of meat.

On cold mornings Sigurd and Aron tried to warm
themselves by the fire, but always the cook drove
them out.

"You are in my way," he said. "How can I work
with you two under my feet!"

When Sigurd and Aron were together, they
talked of many things.

Aron had no father or mother. He liked to hear
stories of Sigurd's home.

Sigurd told him of his mother and father and
sisters. He told him of his cousin Rolf and Old Bard.

"I wish I might see them all," said Aron.

"You shall see them. I'll take you home with me
after the voyage," said Sigurd.

"Do you believe this voyage is taking us to Wineland?" asked Aron.

"Yes," said Sigurd.

"I believe it, too," said Aron. "Gorm is a good man, and he tells the truth."

In their second week at sea, they came in sight of land. It was the shore of Iceland.

Sigurd saw mountains white with ice and snow. He saw green valleys, too, and houses and fields of grain.

The people of Iceland were friendly. They brought food and drink to the men from Norway. There were days and nights of feasting in the homes along the shore.

A boy took Sigurd and Aron to his home. He showed them where springs of hot water rose out of the rocks. He showed them his white bear cub. The cub was tame as a dog. He tried to follow them wherever they went.

Sigurd was happy in Iceland. The other sailors were happy, too. They did not want to leave.

But after a few days Gorm called his men together and said, "We sail tomorrow."

"This is a good land," said Halfred. "Why should we not stay longer?"

"If we stay longer," said Gorm, "we may forget the voyage we have begun."

· "Only three days from now there will be a feast in the town," said Halfred. "Let us stay for the music and dancing."

"We sail tomorrow," said Gorm, "while the wind and weather are fair."

Halfred said nothing more, but his eyes flashed as he looked at Gorm.

11

A Dream of Danger

The ship sailed from Iceland with good winds and fair weather. Life at sea was easy. The men sang and told stories.

In the prow of the ship was a small, high deck. The steersman sat there when he steered the ship. Sometimes Gorm was the steersman. Sigurd liked to sit beside him on the small deck.

Once, for a little while, Sigurd steered the ship. He held the tiller that moved the steering oar.

"It takes a strong hand," he said.

"That it does," said Gorm, as he took the wooden bar again.

He was happy with the ship.

"See how she rides the waves. See how she bites the wind. Another week, and we may be off the Greenland shore."

"I hear that Greenland is a land of ice and snow," said Sigurd.

"This is true," said Gorm.

"Then why must we stop there?" asked Sigurd.

"We can rest there. We can feel the land under our feet," said Gorm. "We can mend the ship if she needs mending. When we sail again, the new land will not be far."

His eyes shone as he spoke. He looked out across the water, almost as if he could see the new land ahead.

For a week the good winds held. Then there was a change in the weather. The winds died. The men went back to the oars.

For days they sailed through fog. It was cold and wet. It soaked the men's clothing. Now and then a little sunlight came through the fog. In the light, the men's faces looked yellow and strange.

One night the ship ran into a storm. Waves came crashing over the deck. Water poured into the rooms below.

Someone cried out, "We are sinking!"

Sigurd heard Gorm shouting above the roar of the storm. "Bail the water! Every man of you, bail!"

Someone put a bailing scoop into Sigurd's hand. He began to scoop up water and pour it into a tub. All about him men were bailing with scoops and buckets. Others were carrying the tubs of water up on deck and pouring them over the sides.

The sailors worked until morning. By that time, most of the storm had passed. The ship was saved.

But one of the men was lost.

Sometime in the night he had gone over the side.

The men spoke of him, their voices low. He was a good man, they said. He left a wife and children at home.

The next morning Sigurd and Gorm were together on the steering deck. Halfred came up and stood between them. He said, "We must turn back."

"What are you saying!" cried Gorm.

"We must turn toward home," said Halfred. "Last night I dreamed of the man who was lost. He spoke to me in his dream. He said, 'There are dangers ahead!'"

"Because of a dream you would turn back?" said Gorm.

"Yes!" said Halfred. "The ship is mine, and now I tell you to turn her toward home."

"The ship is yours, it is true," said Gorm, "but on this voyage I am captain."

"Not any longer!" Halfred caught hold of the tiller. He tried to pull it away from Gorm.

"Take your hands away," said Gorm. There was a look in his eyes that made Halfred draw back.

Sigurd saw him go below.

"You heard what was said?" asked Gorm.

"Yes," said Sigurd.

"Try to forget," said Gorm. "It is better forgotten."

12
Fog and Storm

There were more days of fog. There were days of wind and rain.

One night Sigurd and Aron were rowing side by side. Aron said, "Our captain talks more with you than with anyone else. What does he say of Greenland?"

"What do you mean?" asked Sigurd.

"A week ago he told us we would soon land in Greenland," said Aron. "Now he tells us we are far from there. Why is this?"

"In the fog, we missed Greenland," said Sigurd. "The wind drove us to the south."

"Then where are we now?" asked Aron.

"South of Greenland, and sailing west," said Sigurd. "Our captain has told us this. Do you not believe him?"

"I believe him," said Aron, "but some of the men do not."

"What do they say?" asked Sigurd.

"They say our captain does not know how to steer the ship," said Aron. "They say we are lost."

"Does Halfred say this?"

"Halfred, yes, and others," said Aron.

"Halfred is afraid. He wishes to turn back," said Sigurd. "Would you follow him or Gorm?"

"I would follow Gorm," said Aron, "but all the men do not feel the same."

Another rower came to take Sigurd's place. Sigurd went below to rest and sleep.

It was morning when he woke. Someone was shouting. He ran up the ladder. Halfred was on deck, with a crowd of men about him.

Halfred was breathing hard. There was a wild look in his eyes. "It came to me again—the dream!" he cried. "A man rose out of the waves. He held up his hand and spoke to me."

"What were his words?" asked one of the sailors fearfully.

"His words were 'Turn back!' " said Halfred.

Gorm was on the steering deck. He called Ivar to take the tiller. He came down to where the men were talking.

"I, too, have had dreams," he said. "So have we all."

"But this was a dream of danger," said Halfred. "A man rose out of the sea. His eyes were terrible, and he said, 'Turn back!' "

"How did you answer him?" asked Gorm.

"Answer him?" said Halfred. "How could I answer?"

"When this terrible man next comes to you in a dream, speak up," said Gorm. "Tell him we are not afraid. Tell him we will not turn back until the captain gives the word."

Halfred turned pale with anger.

Some of the men laughed at the joke Gorm had made of Halfred's dream.

But there were more who did not laugh.

Late that afternoon Gorm was back at the tiller. Sigurd went up to the steering deck and spoke to

him. "May I sleep by the door of your room to-night?"

"Why?" asked Gorm.

"I will keep watch," said Sigurd.

"You think I am in danger?" asked Gorm.

"Yes," said Sigurd.

"I have seen the men talking together. I have heard them whisper," said Gorm. "It means nothing. Once we are on land, this will be forgotten."

"The men say we are lost," said Sigurd.

"We are not lost," said Gorm. "Land is near. I have seen land birds, and—" He stopped. He was looking straight before him.

"What is it?" asked Sigurd.

"Look," said Gorm. "Just below the sun."

Sigurd looked. There were a few clouds below the sun. And there was something long and dark that was not a cloud.

"Is it—?" he began.

"*Yes!*" said Gorm.

"Land!" said Sigurd. Then he shouted it, "Land! Land!"

13
"Remember This Day"

The men put out the oars and began to row. Just after sundown a strong wind filled the sail. Still the sailors kept rowing. With the wind in the sail and men at the oars, the ship almost seemed to fly.

Sigurd took his turn. He rowed for half the night. The rest of the night he stayed on deck, waiting for morning.

The sky grew light. He saw the land again, much nearer now. All gray it was, at first.

The sailors were pointing and shouting. But when the sun came up and shone on the land, they grew quiet. They looked in wonder at the shore and the forests beyond. The shore was golden against the bright water. The forests were all the colors of autumn—yellow and brown and red.

Aron said, "See. See the red of the trees—just

like fire. What a beautiful land is this Wineland!"

"See the little harbor," said Ivar. "We can anchor there."

They sailed into the harbor. When the ship lay at anchor, Gorm spoke.

"Some of us will go ashore. Some must stay to guard the ship. Those who go ashore must be armed. In this strange land, there may be danger."

The ship carried two small boats. One was put over the side. Gorm chose a dozen sailors to go ashore with him. Sigurd was among them.

They rowed away. Gorm said to Sigurd, "Remember this day. All that you see and do you may sometime tell your father. So remember it well."

They reached shore and pulled the boat up on the sand. "We must keep together," said Gorm.

They walked through the tall grass along the shore. With their shields held before them, they started into the woods.

One of the men had been a farmer in Norway. He took a stick and dug under the leaves and grass.

"Look at this." He held up a handful of black

earth. "Think of the grain that would grow here!"

They walked on. The woods were still until a bird began to sing.

"There is peace here," said Gorm. "A man might wish to stay forever."

"Does no one live here?" asked Sigurd.

They watched for roads and houses. They saw none.

Beside a stream they lay down and drank the cold, fresh water.

"It is time we turned back," said Gorm. "The rest will be waiting to set foot on shore."

On the way back they saw deer. They saw a bird such as they had never seen before. It was as large as a goose. Its feathers were brown, and its tail spread like a fan. As it ran, it made a rattling sound.

"Now we know," said one of the men. "There is game in these woods."

They came to the shore. The small boat was there where they had left it. And now the ship's other boat was on the sand beside it.

"There were those on the ship who could not

wait," said Gorm. "Well—I cannot blame them."

Sigurd looked at the tracks in the sand. "I see where the men walked. They went into the woods on the far side of the harbor."

"We need not wait for them," said Gorm. "Come, let us go back—"

He stopped, listening.

In the woods someone was shouting.

"Is it not Halfred?" said Gorm.

A band of men came out of the woods. Halfred was leading them. They were running. One man

fell in the tall grass. Another stopped to help him.

Halfred ran far ahead of the others.

"To the boats!" he cried.

"What has happened?" asked Gorm.

"We were set upon!" said Halfred.

"*Who* set upon you?" asked Gorm.

"The savages!" said Halfred.

"Savages—here?" said Gorm.

"Yes. We were in the woods," Halfred told him, "when arrows began to fly past us. We saw the savages on every side."

"Did you not fight back?" asked Gorm.

"Yes," said Halfred, "but they would not stand and fight us, man to man. They hid behind trees. We made a circle and put up our shields. It was only this that saved us."

"You lost no men?" asked Gorm.

"No," said Halfred. "Some were hit by arrows, but they kept to their feet. They are here with the rest."

He looked back, and his face turned pale.

A man had come out of the woods. He was tall and straight. The sun shone on his black hair and red-brown skin. He wore an animal hide about his waist.

He raised his fist and shook it. Then he disappeared into the forest.

"That savage—he is their leader," said Halfred. "He has gone to bring the others."

Gorm said to the men who had gathered about him, "Quick—to the ship."

And very quickly the two boats put out from shore.

14
A String of Shells

Two men were wounded. Back on the ship they were cared for and put to bed.

The others sat on deck. Under a tent of sailcloth they ate their evening meal.

Aron had not gone ashore. He sat down by Sigurd and asked, "Did you see the savages?"

"Only one," said Sigurd.

"Did you see the necklace?" asked Aron.

"What necklace?" asked Sigurd.

"I heard the men telling of it," said Aron. "They told of a necklace that Halfred took from a savage."

Others were talking of the necklace. Their words came to Gorm's ears.

He said to Halfred, "You have not told me of this."

"It is not worth the telling," said Halfred.

"I think it may be," said Gorm. "We are waiting to hear."

Halfred began slowly. "In the woods we came upon three savages. They were the first we had seen. Three young men, they were. One of them wore a necklace."

"And then?" asked Gorm.

"They ran," said Halfred. "I called out to them to stop. They would not. That was why I drew my bow against them."

"You drew your bow against them while they were running away?" asked Gorm.

"Yes, I did," said Halfred. "I brought down the one who wore the necklace."

Gorm sat up straight. "You killed the man?"

"Yes," said Halfred.

"But why?" asked Gorm.

"I told you—he wore a necklace," said Halfred. "I thought it was made of pearls—the largest pearls I had ever seen. But then I found it was worth nothing. It was only a string of white shells. I threw it away."

"You killed him for a string of shells?" said Gorm.

"If they *had* been pearls," said Halfred, "I would be as rich as a king."

"So this is why these people did battle," said Gorm. "They might have been our friends. Now they are sure to be our enemies."

Halfred got to his feet. "In my place you would have done the same. Yet now you blame me."

"Enough," said Gorm. "This is not the time or place to quarrel."

"You will listen to me!" said Halfred. "Long ago I knew there was a curse on this voyage. Now I tell you there is a curse on this land. If you are wise, you will turn toward home. You will not stay another day in the shadow of this land."

Gorm was on his feet, and he stood taller than Halfred. "We have come a long way," he said. "I am not ready to leave so soon. This is a good land. I have seen only a small part of it, and I mean to see more."

He told them of his plan. They would sail from this shore where the savages were their enemies.

They would sail to a farther shore where they were not known.

"We will build houses with a high fence around them," he said. "There we will be safe, if the savages should come."

"Are we to stay there always?" asked a sailor.

"No," said Gorm. "Only until spring. The voyage was long, and winter will soon come upon us. If we sail for home now, winter storms will catch us in the open sea."

"No!" shouted Halfred. "We shall not stay in this land. My dreams have told me—"

"*Enough!*" said Gorm.

The two men looked into each other's eyes, and Halfred was the first to look away.

15
The Cliff

They sailed in the morning. Gorm steered toward the south.

For two days they sailed, always in sight of the shore. On the morning of the third day they came to the mouth of a river.

The sea was rough. A sharp wind blew.

They sailed up the river and anchored there out of the wind.

On both sides were high, rocky cliffs. Gorm looked up at them as if he were pleased.

Since the quarrel, Halfred had kept to his room. Now he came up on deck.

He spoke to Gorm as if they had never quarreled. "Why are we anchored?"

"I like the look of these cliffs," said Gorm. "This may be the spot for our winter home."

"Shall we go ashore together?" asked Halfred.

"Yes, if you wish," said Gorm.

They put out in one of the small boats—Gorm, Halfred, and a party of sailors. Sigurd was among them.

They rowed until they came to a break in the cliffs. They left the boat there and climbed up through the break.

When they reached the woods above, they walked quietly. They listened and watched. But they saw no savages. They saw no signs of any.

Some of the men wanted to look for food.

"See what wild game you can find," said Gorm. "Look for green herbs, too. But take care. Let us stay so close that we can hear one another call." He said to Sigurd, "Shall we explore together? Shall we explore along the cliff?"

"I am ready," said Sigurd.

Halfred came up behind them. "I am coming, too," he said to Gorm. "It will be good for the men to see us walking together. They will know that there is no longer a quarrel between us."

They walked along the cliff. Far below was the river. The water was gray, the color of the sky.

They climbed to a rocky point.

"Here is the place for our winter home," said Gorm. "Here we can keep watch on all sides."

"Yes," said Halfred. "No enemy can surprise us here."

"A high fence on one side will keep us safe," said Gorm. "Next to the cliff we need no fence. No enemy could climb this cliff."

"No," said Halfred. "No one could climb it."

"And these rocks," said Gorm, "we can use when we build our houses."

Halfred had put his hand to his belt. He looked from side to side.

"Is something lost?" asked Gorm.

"Yes. My knife with the white bone handle. It was here in my belt. Now it is gone." Halfred said to Sigurd, "Your eyes are sharp. Go back and see if you can find it."

Sigurd did not want to go. He wanted to stay and explore with Gorm.

But Gorm said nothing. He had turned his back and was busy laying stones to mark where the fence would go.

So Sigurd walked back. Farther and farther he walked, as he looked on the ground for Halfred's knife.

While he was looking among the rocks and grass, he heard a sound. He listened.

The sound came again, louder than before. It was a terrible cry. It was Gorm crying, *"Sigurd!"*

Sigurd's mouth went dry. He turned and began to run.

He ran back along the cliff to where he had left Halfred and Gorm.

"Gorm—" began Sigurd. "He called me. Halfred, where is Gorm!"

Halfred said nothing. He was looking over the cliff.

Sigurd drew near the edge. He looked down.

Far below, between the river and the foot of the cliff, was a strip of rocky sand. There on the rocks lay Gorm.

16
The Knife

Halfred called the men out of the woods.

"A savage has struck!" he said. "Our leader lies dead at the foot of the cliff."

Some of the men looked at one another. Some looked over the cliff.

Ivar drew his sword. "The savage—where has he gone?"

"Did you not see him?" asked Halfred.

"No," said Ivar.

"He ran into the woods," said Halfred. "I was walking ahead, when I heard Gorm's voice. I turned just as the savage struck him down."

"Was the savage alone?" asked Ivar.

"Yes," said Halfred, "but there may be more near-by. Come, let us do quickly what must be done."

He led the men back to the small boat. Sigurd

followed them. Once he stumbled and fell. When he got up, his hand was bleeding. He began to weep, but not from pain. He wept because Gorm was dead.

He got into the boat with the others. He helped row to the foot of the cliff.

Halfred said to him, "You look ill. Stay in the boat," and Sigurd stayed.

The others knelt on the strip of land between the cliff and the river. With knives and their bare hands, they dug a grave.

They buried Gorm along with his sword and shield. They piled stones over the grave.

Halfred said, "Let us go."

They rowed back to the ship.

Evening had come.

"We sail tonight," said Halfred.

"Sail? Where?" asked Ivar.

"For home," said Halfred.

"The voyage will be long," said Ivar. "We need to make ready."

"We must not wait. There is a curse on this

land," said Halfred. "Can you not see there is nothing here—only rocks and trees and cruel savages? While we stay, we are all in danger. Now that Gorm is gone, I am captain, and I say we sail tonight!"

Some of the men gave a cheer. "We sail tonight. Our captain has said it."

Sigurd felt a sickness inside him. So soon they were ready to follow a new captain. So quickly they had begun to forget Gorm.

Some of the men began to talk to him of what had happened that day. He did not want to talk.

He went below and into Gorm's room where he could be alone.

The room was dark and cold. He found Gorm's sleeping bag and pulled it over him. After a while he went to sleep.

When he woke there was a dim light in the room. From under the sleeping bag, he saw a hand hang a lantern on a peg by the door. It was Halfred's hand.

Halfred went away. Almost at once he was back,

with an armload of clothing and a small wooden chest. Gorm's room was the largest and best on the ship. Now that Halfred had made himself captain, he was taking the room for his own.

Sigurd sat up. Halfred started. He dropped the clothing and the chest.

"Why are you here? Why were you hiding?" he asked in a strange, sharp voice. "The ship has sailed. Go find a place at the oars, and never come into this room again!"

Sigurd moved toward the door and stopped. He was looking into the chest that had fallen open at Halfred's feet. A knife was there—one that Sigurd knew well. It had a white bone handle.

"That knife—" he said. "You told me it was lost."

Halfred looked down at the knife.

"You told me it was lost," Sigurd said again. "You sent me back to find it. But it was *not* lost."

"Go to the oars!" said Halfred.

"You lied to me," said Sigurd, "and I know why."

"To the oars!" said Halfred.

Sigurd did not move. "I know now what you are

and what you have done. The look on your face has told me. You sent me away so that you could be alone with Gorm. *You* struck him down."

"No—it was a savage," said Halfred.

"Why did no one else see the savage? And why did Gorm call to me for help? Why did he not call to you?"

Halfred did not answer.

"There was no savage. It was you. And I'll tell them. I'll tell them all!" Sigurd was at the door.

Halfred caught his arm and flung him back. Sigurd fell. Halfred bent over him, holding him down.

"Do you think I fear you?" he said. "Tell your story, and who will believe you? Without Gorm, you are nothing. And I am captain. No one will take your word against mine."

"Then you must fight me!" Sigurd tried to break free.

"Fool," said Halfred. "A man does not fight a boy. Draw your sword against me, speak one word against me, and my men will cut you down."

Sigurd felt a pain over his heart where Halfred's knee held him fast.

"Do you believe what I say?" Halfred pressed harder with his knee. "Speak. Do you believe me?"

"Yes," said Sigurd.

Halfred let him go.

Sigurd got to his feet. He went to the door and looked back. "You are captain here—I know that well," he said, "but my time will come!"

17
On the Steering Deck

The first days out of Wineland were stormy, and cold rain fell. The men brought large, flat tubs up from the storeroom. They caught rain in the tubs. Soon they had a good store of drinking water.

The men talked of home. They tried to guess how long the voyage would last. Some of them sang songs of their homeland.

Sigurd did not sing. He went quietly about his work. There was grief in his heart when he thought of Gorm.

Sometimes he watched Halfred talking and laughing with the other men. He wanted to shout, "Look on this man. He took our captain's life!"

But he waited. Well he remembered what Halfred had said: "Speak a word against me, and my men will cut you down."

Since the night in Gorm's room, Halfred had not spoken to him.

Then, when they had been a week at sea, Halfred sent for him. It was late at night. A sailor came below and said, "You are wanted on deck."

Half-asleep, Sigurd went up the ladder. He was wanted at the oars, he thought.

But there was no one on the rowing benches. The sea was smooth, and a fair wind filled the sail.

"Sigurd—come," said a voice.

He looked toward the steering deck. Halfred was there alone.

"Come," Halfred said again.

Sigurd climbed to the steering deck.

The stars were bright. In their light he could see Halfred's hand on the tiller. He held it in an odd, stiff way. He had never really learned to steer, thought Sigurd. He took his turn at the tiller only to show that he could steer as well as Gorm.

Sigurd said, "You sent for me?"

"Yes. On such a night, steering is not hard," said Halfred. "Do you wish to learn?"

"Not from you," said Sigurd.

"Can we not be friends?" asked Halfred.

"I am your enemy," said Sigurd.

"And at the end of the voyage, will you speak out against me?" asked Halfred.

"Yes," said Sigurd.

"Then you will never see home again!" Halfred let go of the tiller.

It swung toward Sigurd. It would have struck him and sent him into the sea. But he had seen Halfred's move in time. He had thrown himself upon the deck. The heavy wooden bar passed over his head.

With no hand on the tiller, the ship made a sharp turn.

Sailors came running.

"What has happened?" they asked.

Halfred was righting the ship. "It was the boy. He wanted to steer," he said. "I gave him a lesson." He said to Sigurd, "Go back to bed. The lesson is over—for tonight."

Sigurd went below.

He felt cold. All the rest of the night he lay awake, remembering the look in Halfred's eyes.

18
Sigurd and Aron

The next morning Sigurd looked at the men about him. Every day for weeks he had seen them. Yet how much did he know of them? Was there one he could trust?

There was one man, he thought.

That man was Aron.

He waited until Halfred had gone below. Then he spoke to Aron. "I have something to ask of you."

"Ask what you will," said Aron.

"It must be secret," said Sigurd.

"Secret it will be," said Aron.

"When this voyage is over," said Sigurd, "will you go to my home? Will you tell my father and mother and sisters that I thought of them? Will you tell them I saw the land across the sea?"

Aron said in surprise, "Can you not tell them?"

"The voyage may end without me," said Sigurd.

"How could that be?" asked Aron.

"There is one aboard who does not want me to see home again," said Sigurd.

"Who?" asked Aron.

"If I told you," said Sigurd, "you might be in danger, too."

He went away.

That night Aron put his sleeping bag next to Sigurd's. He whispered in the dark, "I know your enemy."

Sigurd whispered back, "Take care what you say."

"It is safe to talk here," said Aron. "Your enemy is Halfred. Is it not true?"

"How did you know?" asked Sigurd.

"I have seen him look at you," said Aron, "as if he wished to sweep you into the sea."

"And that he may do," said Sigurd.

"Why is he your enemy?" asked Aron.

"I know his secret," said Sigurd. "Listen, and tell

my father this. It was no savage who struck Gorm down. It was Halfred."

Aron was quiet for a while.

Sigurd asked, "Did you hear?"

"I heard," said Aron.

"Do you believe me?" asked Sigurd.

"Yes," said Aron, "but what can I do? How can I help you?"

"I think there is no help for me," said Sigurd.

The ship sailed into storms.

Food ran low.

One day a large fish was washed up on deck.

"The sea sends us our dinner!" said a sailor.

But the fish made no more than a mouthful for each of the men.

Halfred had grown thin. His eyes were staring and strange.

He and Sigurd met on deck one evening. Halfred bent down. He said very softly, so that no one else could hear, "Do not think I have forgotten you, friend of Gorm!"

19
A Light
on the Island

Forty-six days out of Wineland the ship sailed into calm waters. The clouds lifted, and there was land ahead.

Some of the men knew the land. It was one of the Faroe Islands. From the Faroes it was no more than a week's voyage to the homeland.

Ivar spoke from the steering deck. "In these waters there is danger of hidden rocks. But I know a safe harbor on the far side of this island. Shall I steer toward it?"

Sigurd heard the words. A thought came to him. If the ship anchored here, he might escape!

He saw Halfred look at him.

Halfred seemed to read his thought. He said, "We shall not stop here."

"The ship needs mending," said Ivar, "and our food is low."

"There would be little food for us in this poor place," said Halfred. "The ship has brought us this far. It will take us the rest of the way. Besides, the sea is calm. Now is the time to sail home with all speed."

"But a new storm is rising," said Ivar. "I can see it in the sky. I can feel it in the air."

"Why should we fear another storm?" said Halfred. "We shall sail on."

Dark came early.

Sigurd went below and tried to sleep. Aron came down. He put his sleeping bag beside Sigurd's.

"If we had stopped at this island," he whispered, "you might have escaped."

"But now the chance is gone," Sigurd whispered back.

They lay quiet. Someone was coming down the ladder.

A sailor put his head into the room. "Sigurd?" he said.

"Yes," said Sigurd.

"The captain waits for you on the steering deck," said the sailor.

"Why?" asked Sigurd.

"How should I know?" said the sailor, and he went away.

Aron said, "Do not go!"

"He has sent for me," said Sigurd. "I must go."

"Hide yourself," said Aron.

"There is no place," said Sigurd.

"But if you go to Halfred, you will not come back," said Aron.

"If I stay," said Sigurd, "he will seek me here."

Aron was out of his sleeping bag. "Come," he said. "There may be a way—"

They climbed the ladder.

The main deck was in darkness. Sigurd followed Aron back through the shadows.

Someone spoke, "Who is there?"

It was a sailor on watch.

Aron pushed Sigurd to the deck. "Lie there," he whispered.

Sigurd lay beside one of the big, wooden rain tubs.

Aron said to the man on watch, "Where are you? I cannot see you."

"I am here by the side," said the man. "Have you come looking for me?"

"Yes," said Aron. "I am here to take your place."

"Good," said the man. "I have long been ready to sleep."

Sigurd heard him walk away.

"Stand up," whispered Aron. "Look to the island!"

Sigurd stood up. Far away he saw a light shining like a star.

"You may reach it," said Aron.

"I could not swim so far," said Sigurd.

"No," said Aron, "but in the tub—"

"Yes!" said Sigurd.

Aron had found a rope. He and Sigurd tied it to the handles of the rain tub.

"Hurry," said Aron. "Soon Halfred will come looking for you."

They lifted the tub and let it down over the side of the ship.

"Now," said Aron.

Sigurd climbed over the side. He slid down the rope and into the tub.

Aron let go of the rope. Sigurd felt the tub rock beneath him as a wave caught it and carried it away.

20
The Hut

Sigurd could see nothing except the light on the island. He tried to steer toward it. He put his hand into the water and tried to row.

But there was no way to steer the tub. There was no way to row.

The tub rode the water like a cork. Its tipping and rocking threw Sigurd from side to side.

He was not sure he was drifting toward the island. He could no longer see the light.

He thought, this tub cannot carry me far. It will soon sink or turn over. There is small chance that it will take me to shore.

Yet for the first time in weeks he felt free. He had escaped from the ship. He was out of Halfred's reach.

The wind was rising. The roar of the sea grew

deep and loud. Ivar had said a new storm was in the air. The storm had come.

The tub rose and fell, and rose again. It rode wave after wave.

Then Sigurd felt himself spun around, as if he were caught in a whirlpool. There was a crash and a sound of breaking wood. The tub fell apart.

Sigurd tried to swim. His clothes dragged him down. Numb with cold, he fought to keep his head above water.

He sank, and his feet touched land!

He took a step. A wave pushed him forward, and he fell.

When he picked himself up, he was out of the water. He began to crawl.

Sometimes walking, sometimes crawling, he made his way over rocks and sand.

The wind tore at his clothes. Rain began to fall.

In the darkness he came up against a large rock. He lay down beside it, out of the wind. There he waited for the storm and the night to pass.

When morning broke, the day was still.

Sigurd was stiff with cold. It was hard for him to move. Slowly he got to his feet.

He looked out to sea. There were rocks rising out of the water. The tub had struck one of them.

He began to walk away from the sea. The land was rocky and bare. Among the rocks he saw a long-haired sheep with a bell hanging from its neck. The sheep looked at him and ran away.

Sigurd found a path and followed it. He was warmer now. It was easier for him to walk.

He kept on until he saw someone in the path ahead.

It was a man. He was small and bent and old, and his clothes were all rags and patches.

"Well met," said Sigurd.

"Who are you?" asked the old man. "You are no island boy."

"I came from a ship," said Sigurd.

"Ah, you were in the storm." The old man came close to him. "Are you hurt?"

"No," said Sigurd, "but if you know of a place where I could rest—"

"My home is near," said the old man.

He led the way to a hut on the side of a hill. His wife, as small and bent and old as he, made Sigurd a bed by the fire.

"Now then—now, my fine boy," she kept saying quietly.

Sigurd went to sleep.

When he woke, the hut was full of people. They were looking at him.

"Were you the only one saved?" asked a man.

"Saved?" Sigurd tried to understand.

"Are you not from the Viking ship that was wrecked?" asked the man.

"Wrecked, did you say?" Sigurd sat up.

"Surely you must know the ship was wrecked," said the man.

"Pieces of it are still coming to shore," said another man.

"Where? I must see." Sigurd was on his feet.

"Lie down," said the old woman.

"No. Let me see," said Sigurd.

He went with them to the shore.

They showed him the broken wood and a torn
piece of sailcloth.

"This was my ship," he said. "Was no one
saved?"

"We have seen no one," said a man, "only you."

Sigurd stood there, looking out to sea.

The old man came to his side. "Will you come
with me now?"

And Sigurd went with him back to the hut.

21
Sigurd's Story

The old man and his wife were kind to Sigurd. Poor as they were, they shared their food with him.

He helped them in return. He kept the fire burning. He dug paths in the deep snows.

All through the islands, people spoke of him. "He alone was saved from the wreck," they said. Some of them came to the hut to hear his story.

"I was not aboard when the ship was wrecked," he told them. "The captain was my enemy, and I left the ship to save my life."

"A foolish captain, surely," the people said, "to sail these waters in the time of the winter storms. Where had this voyage taken you?"

"To Wineland," he said.

"Do you mean Greenland?" they asked. Or they asked, "Is Wineland another name for Iceland?"

"No!" he said. "Wineland is a land far beyond."

But he could not make them understand.

In the spring he said good-by to the old man and his wife. He went to the harbor. There in the little town he waited for a ship from home.

One came at last.

Sigurd asked the captain, "Will you take me back to Norway?"

The captain saw that Sigurd was tall and strong. "You may go with us," he said. "We need a rower."

Sigurd told the captain his story. The captain listened and said nothing.

Some of the sailors began to talk of Wineland. "You, Sigurd," they said. "You were there. Tell us how it is."

He saw that they were laughing. They did not believe his story.

He would not answer them. On the week's voyage he did his work, but he said little.

The ship anchored at the port of Kon.

As Sigurd walked through the village, he saw a face he knew. It was the face of his cousin Rolf.

He called to him, "Rolf! Do you remember me? Do you remember the lessons we had together?"

"I remember," said Rolf. He was still not friendly. "Where have you been?"

"To Wineland," said Sigurd. "I shipped with Gorm, and I am the only one to come home."

"All the way to Wineland!" said Rolf. "And since no one else came home, you can tell the story as you like."

Once Sigurd would have fought him for the words. Now he only said, "So you do not believe me. It does not matter. I know what I have seen, and no one can take it from me."

He left the town. He walked by day and slept under the sky by night. People along the way gave him food.

On the second day he came to Torvik. On the third day he came in sight of home.

The dogs barked at him as if he were a stranger.

He carried a stick, and he swung it among them until they drew back. He went up to the house, and a servant looked out at him.

"The young master!" cried the servant. "He is here—the young master!"

Sigurd's sisters came running to the door. Then they stopped and looked at each other. Sigurd saw sadness in their eyes.

"What is it?" he asked.

They put their arms about him and led him inside.

His mother was there.

"Sigurd—I heard your voice, but I could not believe it was you. It is so long since you went away." She asked, "Have the girls told you?"

"Told me what?" he asked.

"Your father—" she began.

He saw the tears on her face.

He asked, "Is my father dead?"

"Yes," she said.

Sigurd asked, "When did he die?"

"Not long after you went away," she said. "His wound had never healed, and—"

"I understand," said Sigurd.

He went into the great hall. It seemed he had

been away for many years. He walked past the shields and swords on the wall.

He stood before his father's chair.

His mother had come into the hall. "We need you, Sigurd. You are the man here now."

"I know, and I shall stay." He asked, "Is Old Bard still with us?"

"Yes," said his mother, "but he is old and very weak."

Sigurd went to the old man's room. Bard was sitting by the window. He was bending over a book, with his face close to the pages.

"Bard!" said Sigurd.

The old man looked up.

"My young friend!" he said. "You have come home!"

"Yes, I have come to stay," said Sigurd.

"Stand in the light," said Bard, "so that I may see you better."

Sigurd went to the window.

Bard gazed at him. "Ah, you have been far. You have had adventures. I see it in your eyes."

"I have had a great adventure." Sigurd looked at the books on the table. "Bard, could *my* story be written? Could it go into a book so that others could read it?"

The old man put out his hands. They had grown stiff. His fingers would hardly bend. "I cannot write it for you," he said.

"Can you teach me writing?" asked Sigurd. "Is it too late?"

"It is not too late," said Bard.

"I shall write my story," said Sigurd. "Many will not believe it. But some day a man will read my words and believe them. He will read of the land I have seen, and he will go there. He will go in peace, and it will be a great land for him."

"Will you tell your story?" asked Bard. "May I hear it now?"

"Yes," said Sigurd.

Together they went into the great hall.

Sigurd's mother and sisters were waiting. Some of the servants had come to the door to watch and listen.

The dragon chair had been drawn up in front of the fire.

Sigurd looked at his mother.

She nodded her head.

He sat down in the chair. For a little while he sat there, thinking. Then he began to tell his story.

About the Author

Clyde Robert Bulla grew up on a farm near King City, Missouri. He received his early education in a one-room schoolhouse where he began writing stories and songs. He finished his first book shortly after his graduation from high school and then went to work on a newspaper as a columnist and a typesetter.

He continued to write, and his books for children became so successful that he was able to satisfy his desire to travel through the United States, Mexico, and Hawaii. His home is in Los Angeles, and it is there that he composes his songs and writes his stories.

About the Illustrator

Douglas Gorsline's paintings and etchings are represented in many collections, and in most national exhibitions, such as those at the Whitney Museum, Chicago Art Institute, the Pennsylvania Academy, the Library of Congress, etc. Among other awards, he has won the Arms and Shope Prizes in the Annual of the Society of American Etchers, and First Prize in the Library of Congress Annual.

Mr. Gorsline studied at the Yale School of Fine Arts and at the Art Students League in New York. He has taught at the National Academy of Design in New York City, and is now actively painting. He is the author and illustrator of the well-known costume history *What People Wore* (Viking).